Tall Tales books bring to the primary reader stories filled with boisterous action, humor, and excitement. Some are based on folklore; others are pure fantasy.

All the books have colorful illustrations that capture to perfection the gay, carefree mood of the text.

Each author has created an imaginative, easy-to-read story designed to entice the reader into the magic realm of books.

The Farmer
and the Witch

By Ida DeLage

Illustrated by Gil Miret

GARRARD PUBLISHING COMPANY
CHAMPAIGN, ILLINOIS

The **Farmer** and the **Witch**

One night
a farmer was out
in his cornfield.
He was looking for his bull.
Some boys had let the bull
out of his pen.

The boys were hiding
in the apple tree.
They laughed so hard
the apple tree shook.
Oh, what a trick this was
on the old farmer!

Suddenly
an old witch flew by
on her broom.
"BOO!" she said.
The boys were so scared
they fell out of the tree.
They ran for home
as fast as their legs
could carry them.

The old farmer
was still looking for the bull.
Just as he passed
a stack of corn,
the old witch jumped out.
"BOO!" she said.
"Boo yourself!"
said the farmer.
He thought the witch was a boy
dressed up in a Halloween mask
and an old black dress.
"If the bull sees you,
he'll toss you over the fence,"
said the farmer.

Oh, that made the witch angry!
Now she would scare this farmer
out of his skin.
She screeched like an owl.
Her eyes glowed like fire.
She blew a puff of smoke
right in the farmer's face.

"Get out of here!"
said the farmer.
"I'll chase you out
with my hayfork."
He chased the old witch
around the corn stack
three times.

The old witch
jumped on her broom
to fly away.
Her foot went
right through a pumpkin.
The pumpkin stuck on her foot
like a big yellow boot.
How that old witch did dance!
She hopped around.
She shook her foot.
The pumpkin wouldn't come off.
So she jumped on her broom,
pumpkin and all.
Off she went!

She had not gone very high
when the heavy pumpkin fell off.
It dropped
right on the bull's head.
The bull gave a snort
and pawed the ground.

He chased the farmer
all around the corn stack.
The bull tossed his head.
The pumpkin flew off his horns.
It flew right into the window
of the farmer's kitchen.

In the morning,
the farmer's wife
found the pumpkin on the table.
She baked it into a golden pie.
That night
the mayor came to dinner.
His eyes lit up,
when he saw the pie.

"Ah," said the mayor.

"My favorite pie."

The farmer's wife

started to cut the pie.

The mayor picked up his fork.

Then . . .

before their very eyes . . .

    ZIP!

The pie flew out the window.

"This is a trick,"
said the mayor.
"A mean, mean trick!"
He ran out of the house.
The farmer ran after him.
"Stop! Stop!
Let me explain!"
the farmer cried.
But who can explain
a flying pumpkin pie?
The old witch
laughed herself silly.
She wiped the pie crumbs
off her hairy old chin.

The old witch
went to her cave.
She made a big pot
of witch's brew.
She stirred it
  slowly . . .
     slowly . . .

She sang a song:

Seven toadstools in a row.

Old black feathers from a crow.

Wiggle worm,

Spider spin,

Drop another lizard in.

Big fat grub,

A snail or two.

Cook them up

For witch's brew.

She stirred it 99 times
to the left.
She stirred it 99 times
to the right.

She said,
    "Ooga ooga
        Booga boo."
The old witch laughed,
"Hee, hee, hee!
This is the best brew
I have ever made."
She put it in a jug.
"Now I will put a spell
on that old farmer
that he will never forget."

The old witch jumped
on her broom.
Up into the sky she flew!
The old witch flew fast.
She did a dive.
She did a loop-the-loop.
Even the bats got
out of her way.

Then,
just as she made a turn
to zip over the barn,
         SMACK!
She bumped into the silo!
Her hat flew off.
Her broom crumpled up.

The old witch fell
right into the watering trough.
But worst of all,
her jug broke
into a million, billion pieces.

And her best magic
witch's brew
fell like rain
all over the barnyard.
The old witch
got out of the water.
She climbed on her
poor old broom.
She flew back
to her cave
and hid.

In the morning
the farmer began
to milk his cow.
The cow stood
on her head.
The chickens laid
polka-dot eggs.
The bull was scared
by a bumblebee
and stuck his head
in the haystack.

The sheep's wool
was all tied up
in knots.
The horse kicked
the plow up into
the apple tree.
The goose thought
she was really
a weather vane.
The poor farmer
was at his wit's end.

N   S

The farmer's wife thought,
"Ah-ha!
This must be the work
of an old witch.
My old granny told me
all about witches.
I know what to do!"
She said to the farmer,
"Get busy, old man,
and do as I say.
You must drive
all of the animals
into the barn
   BACKWARDS!"

Well!
Did *you* ever try
to drive a nanny goat
into a barn backwards?

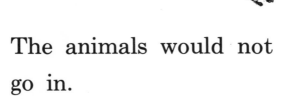

The animals would not
go in.
The farmer scratched
his head.
The farmer's wife
sat down to think.

At last she showed the farmer
what to do.
He took off the barn door.
Then he put it on again
backwards.
The old farmer
drove all of the animals
into the barn.
Then he put the barn door
on again the right way.

The spell was broken.
"Ha-ha! Ho-ho!"
The farmer and his wife
danced the higgety-jig
all around the barnyard.
"We are smarter than
any old witch,"
they sang.

But . . .

In her dark cave

the witch was stirring something.

And she had another jug.

"Ooga ooga

Booga boo.

I'll fix that farmer yet,"

said the old witch.

She put in

two extra spiders—very hairy.

She stirred it 100 times

to the right.

She put in

three extra toadstools.

She stirred it 100 times
to the left.
She said,
"Ooga ooga booga boo
BOO!"
A big puff of smoke
came out of the pot.

Even the old witch
got scared.
This was the most magic brew
there ever was.
When the old witch
put the brew in the jug,
the cork blew off
three times.

At last the brew was ready.
The witch put the jug
under her arm.
Then she got on her broom
and flew right to the barnyard.
This time
she was very careful.
She didn't do one trick.
She didn't go near the silo.
She went right to the well.
It was dark.
She poured all of the brew
into the well,

Glug—glug—glug.

"Hee hee hee!"
cackled the old witch.
"Wait until the farmer
takes a drink of that!"
Then she hopped on her broom.
She flew back to her cave
and took a nap.

The next morning
the farmer went to the well
to get some water.
He began to water his garden.
The rosebush grew onions.
The bluebells started to ring.
The pumpkins
turned into jack-o'-lanterns.
The peach tree grew pickles.
The weeping willow
started to laugh.
The corn began to pop.
Worms came out of their holes
and began to dance.

"By gollys!

That old witch is back again,"

said the farmer.

He ran to tell his wife.

But it was too late.

The farmer's wife

was drinking tea.

She had made it

from the well-water.

Already her nose

was a foot long.

The farmer's wife

got her book

about magic spells.

She read:

"What to do about

    WELL SPELLS:

Find a pink-eyed hoppy toad

and put it down the well."

So the old farmer and his wife

went looking for hoppy toads.

They found 45 hoppy toads.

But *not one* had pink eyes.

There was one old toad left.

It was asleep on a stone

in the sun.

The farmer poked the hoppy toad.
It would not wake up.
"Wake up!"
said the farmer.
He gave the hoppy toad
another poke.
The hoppy toad opened one eye.
Sure enough! It was pink!
The toad opened the other eye.
That one was pink too.

"Good!" said the farmer.
He took the pink-eyed toad
and dropped it down the well.
It drank up all the witch's brew.
Pink-eyed hoppy toads
love witches' brew.
That's why
you always see hoppy toads
around witches' caves.
Now the spell was broken.

That night
the farmer went out
to his cornfield.
He was waiting
for the old witch.
"Boo!"
The old witch jumped out.
"Boo back!" said the farmer.

He chased the witch
all around the corn stack.
The farmer stuck his hayfork
through the witch's black cloak.
"Eeeeeek!"
screeched the witch.
She jumped right out
of her cloak and flew away.

"Ha, ha!" laughed the farmer.
"Now I'm sure I'll never see
that old witch again.
Ho, ho, ho!"
The old farmer laughed so hard
he fell over backwards.

The farmer took the cloak
and stuffed it with straw.
"This will make
a fine scarecrow," he said.
And he put it in his cornfield.
Then the happy farmer
went to bed.

Outside, the moon was shining
like a big yellow pumpkin
in the sky.
But the old farmer
did not see a thing.
He just snored
    and snored
        and snored.